To my amazing nephews, Gabe, Fred, Hugo, David, and Mark—
and my new niece or nephew who is on the way. . . . —M.O.

For Uncle Bruce —A.J.

The Legend of King Arthur-a-tops
Text copyright © 2020 by Mo O'Hara
Illustrations copyright © 2020 by Andrew Joyner
All rights reserved. Manufactured in China.
No part of this book may be used or reproduced in any manner whatsoever without written permission
except in the case of brief quotations embodied in critical articles and reviews. For information address
HarperCollins Children's Books, a division of HarperCollins Publishers, 195 Broadway, New York, NY 10007.
www.harpercollinschildrens.com
ISBN 978-0-06-265275-1
The artist used Procreate and Adobe Photoshop to create the digital illustrations for this book.
Typography by Chelsea C. Donaldson
19 20 21 22 23 SCP 10 9 8 7 6 5 4 3 2 1

First Edition

THE LEGEND OF KING ARTHUR-A-TOPS

by Mo O'Hara   illustrated by Andrew Joyner

HARPER
An Imprint of HarperCollinsPublishers

Once upon a time, 150 million years ago, in the misty swamps of Camelot, there lived three young dino squires training to be knights.

Lancelot-o-saur was strong and brave.

Guinevere-raptor was fast and fearless.

And Arthur-a-tops was . . . well . . . he was just Arthur-a-tops.

It was the Festival of the Stone, and knight-o-saurs came from all over the kingdom to try to pull the golden-ringed dinosaur horn from the magical stone.

Whoever succeeded would be crowned king or queen.

"Who will pull the horn, Rex-calibur, from the stone?"
Merlin-a-dactyl said, hovering over the crowd.

"Nobody," Lancelot-o-saur mumbled.

"No one ever does," Guinevere-raptor agreed.

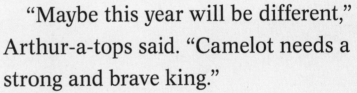

"Maybe this year will be different," Arthur-a-tops said. "Camelot needs a strong and brave king."

Guinevere-raptor growled. "Or a fast and fearless queen, of course," she said.

One by one the knight-o-saurs
tried to pull the horn.

They tugged and twisted.
They thwacked and thumped.

One knight even tried sitting on the stone to hatch it like an egg, but no luck.

One by one, they all failed.

"Why can't any of them do it?" Arthur-a-tops wondered.

Merlin-a-dactyl swooped out of the mist and hovered over Arthur-a-tops.

"None of them are the one true king," he whispered.

"Dino squires! Come at once," Sir Stomps-a-lot demanded. "Fetch our horn-tipped lances for the joust!"

"We better go," Lancelot-o-saur said. "You coming, Arthur-a-tops?" Guinevere-raptor asked.

"Yeah," Arthur-a-tops answered. "I just need to remember where I put the lance."

He had used the lance to
help a few dinos earlier.

There was that pterodactyl
he'd got back up into his tree . . .

the stegosaurus who'd
needed her back scratched . . .

and the iguanodon who needed
a toothpick.

"Aha!" Arthur-a-tops said, spotting the lance next to the iguanodon's toothbrush. But the horn tip was broken and covered in half-chewed pieces of fern.

EEWWWW

"I need my lance!" the knight yelled. "Now!!!"
Arthur-a-tops looked around, quickly grabbed the first horn tip he saw, and pulled.

Ziiiinnng!

A gasp came up from the crowd.

"Look! Arthur-a-tops pulled the horn from the stone!" Guinevere-raptor shouted.

The crowd laughed.
"That little dino?"
"He's not a king!"

Down swooped Merlin-a-dactyl. "Who doubts that this young dinosaur is the one true king?"

Every dinosaur raised its hand,
except for the ones with tiny arms,
who just nodded and said, "Me."
"He's so small."
"He's only a squire."
"He could never be our king."

"I'm so sorry, everyone,"
Arthur-a-tops mumbled.
"I'll put it back."

tumbled,

But he tripped over his tail,

and crashed headfirst
into the magic stone.

Ziiinnnng!

"Ummm, I think I'm stuck."

"Seriously?" Guinevere-raptor asked. "Only you could get your own horn stuck in the magic stone!"

Once again, all the knight-o-saurs
tried and tried to pull out the horn.

They tugged and twisted.
They thwacked and thumped.
Thankfully, no one tried to sit
on Arthur-a-tops to hatch him.

"You have to believe that you are the one true king, Arthur-a-tops," said Merlin-a-dactyl. "*You* are the only one who can free yourself."

"And what if I can't?" Arthur-a-tops asked.

"Then you are going to have to build up some strong neck muscles to carry that rock around!"

"I can't be the one true king. I'm only a dino squire. . . ." Arthur-a-tops started to say.

"And a bit forgetful," Lancelot-o-saur said.

"And kinda clumsy," Guinevere-raptor added.

"Arthur-a-tops helps everyone, and that is the mark of a true king. I believe you can do it, Arthur-a-tops."

"Me too," said Lancelot-o-saur. "So what if you're forgetful? You never forget to be a good friend."

"And so what if you're clumsy? You literally fall over yourself to help other dinos. I believe in you, too," said Guinevere-raptor. "Just watch where you drop the stone when you take it off, okay?"

Arthur-a-tops looked around at the whole crowd of dinosaurs and tried to believe. He took a deep breath and heaved.

In one tug he freed his horn from the stone.
And when it emerged, it was gilded in golden rings!

Merlin-a-dactyl crowned Arthur-a-tops as the one true king. There was much rejoicing throughout Camelot.

That was . . . **Until. . .**